The Night Before Christmas

The Night Before Christmas

Written by
Clement Clarke Moore

Illustrated by
Donald Mills

ideals children's books®
Nashville, Tennessee

ISBN-13: 978-0-8249-5627-1

Published by Ideals Children's Books
An imprint of Ideals Publications
A Guideposts Company
Nashville, Tennessee
www.idealsbooks.com

Color separations by Precision Color Graphics, Franklin, Wisconsin

Printed and bound in China

Library of Congress Cataloging-in-Publication Data

Moore, Clement Clarke, 1779–1863.
  The night before Christmas / written by Clement Clarke Moore ; illustrated by Donald Mills.
      p. cm.
  "An Ideals Christmas classic."
            (pbk. : alk. paper)
  1. Santa Claus—Juvenile poetry. 2. Christmas—Juvenile poetry. 3. Children's poetry, American. I. Mills, Donald, 1896–1974, ill. II. Title.
  PS2429.M5N5 2005
  811'.2—dc22
                          2005009109

Cover illustration by George Hinke
Designed by Marisa Jackson

Leo_Jul10_1

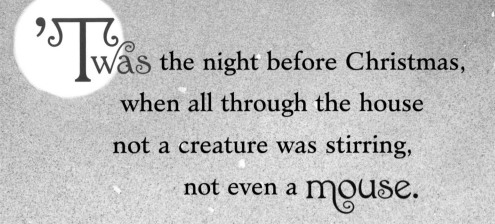

'Twas the night before Christmas,
when all through the house
not a creature was stirring,
not even a mouse.

The stockings were hung
by the chimney with care
in hopes that Saint Nicholas
soon would be there.

The children were nestled
all snug in their beds,
while visions of sugarplums
danced in their heads.

And Mama in her kerchief
and I in my cap
had just settled our brains
for a long winter's nap.

When out on the lawn there arose such a clatter,
I sprang from my bed to see what was the matter.
Away to the window I flew like a flash,
tore open the shutters, and threw up the sash.

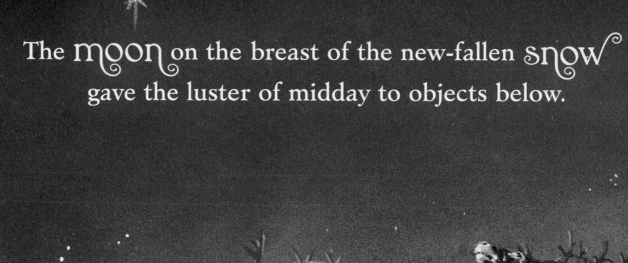

The MOON on the breast of the new-fallen SNOW
gave the luster of midday to objects below.

When what to my wondering eyes should appear,
but a miniature sleigh
and eight tiny reindeer,

With a little old driver
so lively and quick,
I knew in a moment
it must be Saint Nick.

More rapid than eagles
his coursers they came,
and he whistled and shouted
and called them by name.

"Now, Dasher! Now, Dancer!
Now, Prancer and Vixen!
On, Comet! On, Cupid!
On, Donder and Blitzen!

"To the top of the porch!
To the top of the wall!
Now, dash away! Dash away!
Dash away, all!"

As dry leaves that before the wild hurricane fly
when they meet with an obstacle, mount to the sky,
so up to the housetop the coursers they flew,
with the sleigh full of toys
and Saint Nicholas too.

And then, in a twinkling, I heard on the roof
the prancing and pawing of each little hoof.
As I drew in my head and was turning around,
down the chimney Saint Nicholas
came with a bound.

He was dressed all in fur
from his head to his foot,
and his clothes were all
tarnished
with ashes and soot.
A bundle of toys
he had flung on his back,
and he looked like a
peddler
just opening his pack.

His eyes—how they twinkled!
His dimples—how merry!
His cheeks were like roses,
his nose like a cherry!

His droll little mouth was drawn up like a bow,
and the beard of his chin was as white as the snow.

The stump of a pipe he held tight in his teeth,
and the smoke, it encircled his head like a wreath.

He had a broad face
and a little round belly
that shook when he laughed,
like a bowl full of jelly.

He was chubby and plump,
a right jolly old elf,
and I laughed when I saw him
in spite of myself.

A wink of his eye
and a twist of his head
soon gave me to know
I had nothing to dread.

He spoke not a word, but went straight to his work,
and filled all the stockings; then turned with a jerk,
and laying his finger aside of his nose,
and giving a nod, up the chimney he rose.

He sprang to his sleigh,
to his team gave a whistle,
and away they all flew like the down of a thistle.

But I heard him exclaim
ere he drove out of sight,

"Happy Christmas
to all, and
to all a good night!"